Anonymous

Thirty-Second Annual Report of the Directors of James Murray's Royal Asylum for Lunatics

Anatiposi

Anonymous

Thirty-Second Annual Report of the Directors of James Murray's Royal Asylum for Lunatics

Reprint of the original.

1st Edition 2023 | ISBN: 978-3-38230-470-6

Anatiposi Verlag is an imprint of Outlook Verlagsgesellschaft mbH.

Verlag (Publisher): Outlook Verlag GmbH, Zeilweg 44, 60439 Frankfurt, Deutschland
Vertretungsberechtigt (Authorized to represent): E. Roepke, Zeilweg 44, 60439 Frankfurt, Deutschland
Druck (Print): Books on Demand GmbH, In de Tarpen 42, 22848 Norderstedt, Deutschland

THIRTY-SECOND

ANNUAL REPORT

OF THE

DIRECTORS

OF

JAMES MURRAY'S ROYAL ASYLUM

FOR

LUNATICS,

NEAR PERTH.

JUNE, 1859.

PERTH:
THE PERTH PRINTING COMPANY: W. BELFORD, PRINTER.

MDCCCLIX.

LIST OF OFFICE-BEARERS.

1859-60.

WILLIAM PEDDIE, Esq. of Blackruthven, *Chairman.*

DIRECTORS.

I.—EX-OFFICIO.

The Right Hon. the Earl of Kinnoull, Lord-Lieutenant of the County of Perth.
Edward Strathearn Gordon, Esq. Sheriff of the County of Perth.
Hugh Barclay, Esq. LL.D. Sheriff-Substitute of the County of Perth.
William Imrie, Esq. Lord Provost of the City of Perth.
David Stuart, Esq. Dean of Guild of said City.
John Kemp, Esq. First Bailie of said City.
James Spottiswoode, Esq. President of the Society of Procurators, Perth.
Peter Tait, Esq. Convener of the Trades of Perth.
The Rev. John Elder Cumming, Minister of the East Church, Perth.

II.—LIFE DIRECTORS.

William Peddie, Esq. of Blackruthven.
Major-General John Murray Belshes, Invermay House.
John Beatson Bell, Esq. of Glenfarg.
John Marshall, Esq. of Rosemount, Perth.

III.—ANNUAL DIRECTORS.

The Right Honourable the Earl of Mansfield.
The Right Honourable Lord Rollo.
William Smythe, Esq. of Methven.
David Wedderspoon, Esq. Solicitor, Perth.
William Thomson, Esq. of Balgowan.
J. M. Nairne, Esq. of Dunsinnan.
D. L. Jolly, Esq. Banker, Perth.
Archibald Turnbull, Esq. of Bellwood.
Sir Thomas Moncreiffe of Moncreiffe, Baronet.
John Murray Drummond, Esq. of Megginch.
Charles Graham Sidey, Esq. Perth.
William Ross, Esq. Solicitor, Perth.

COMMITTEES.

I.—WEEKLY COMMITTEE.

William Peddie, Esq.
Major-General Belshes.
Archibald Turnbull, Esq.
David Wedderspoon, Esq.
D. L. Jolly, Esq.
Sir Thomas Moncreiffe.
John Marshall, Esq.
William Ross, Esq.

II.—HOUSE VISITING COMMITTEE.

William Peddie, Esq. | Major-General Belshes. | John Marshall, Esq.

William Malcom, Esq. M.D. *Physician.*
W. Lauder Lindsay, Esq. M.D. *Resident Medical Superintendent.*
John Lorimer, Esq. M.D. *Resident Medical Assistant.*
The Rev. Robert James Craig, *Chaplain.*
Messrs. Mackenzie & Dickson, Solicitors, Perth, *Joint Secretaries* and *Treasurers.*
Messrs. J. & R. Morison, Accountants, Perth, *Auditors.*
Miss Matilda Giddings, *Matron.*
Miss Ann Muirhead Shearer, *Housekeeper.*

ANNUAL REPORT

BY THE DIRECTORS OF

JAMES MURRAY'S ROYAL ASYLUM

FOR LUNATICS.

13TH JUNE, 1859.

It is now the duty of the Directors to submit the Thirty-Second Annual Report of the Institution.

At the date of the last Annual Report there were in the House 175 patients—84 males and 91 females. Since then, 79 patients have been admitted—37 males and 42 females. The total number of patients under treatment during the year, was 254—121 males and 133 females. Of this number 34 have recovered—13 males and 21 females; 3 were removed improved—2 males and 1 female; 5 were removed unimproved—1 male and 4 females; and 11 have died—7 males and 4 females. There now remain in the Asylum 201 patients—98 males and 103 females—a greater number considerably than at any former period in the history of the Institution. For the ages of the patients admitted during the past year, the form of their insanity, its causes, duration, and other particulars, reference is made to the report of the Medical Superintendent and Appendix thereto, hereto subjoined.

It is gratifying to the Directors to observe, that during the past year the Institution has continued to enjoy the confidence of the public, evinced not only by the extra number of patients who have been admitted, but by no less than 74 patients having been refused admission from want of accommodation. As usual, they have also to record a good proportion of cures effected during the year, and in most instances arising in cases subjected to early treatment, which, while a pleasing consideration in itself, should operate as an inducement to the friends and guardians of the insane to secure for them, at the earliest possible stage of their malady, the advantages of a good Asylum.

Since the last Annual Meeting, Dr. Lindsay, as sanctioned by the Directors, has taken up his residence at Pitcullen Bank, and the services of Dr. Lorimer have been obtained as Assistant Superintendent, and these arrangements have been attended with the happiest effects.

The Report of the Medical Superintendent enters both ably and fully into many practical details as to the working of the Institution, which will no doubt be read with advantage not only by professional men, but also by those who take an interest in the treatment and cure of the insane, and to it the Directors would invite particular attention.

In conclusion, the Directors, while feeling thankful for the success which has heretofore attended the Institution, trust, through the Divine blessing, it may long continue to confer important benefits on the community.

REPORT

BY

MEDICAL SUPERINTENDENT

FOR THE YEAR, 1858-9.

At no former period in the history of the Institution has its population been so great as it is at present, or as it has been during the greater part of the past year. At the present date it is represented by 201 residents: but it has been so high as 204, while the total number of patients under treatment during the year has been 254. The number of residents at the date of the last annual meeting was 175: so that there is an increase in favour of the present date of 26 patients.

General Results of Year.

Maximum Population.

79 patients were admitted during the year: that is 10 in excess of the previous year. But this increase in the number of admissions by no means adequately represents the great demand made on our accommodation during the past year. In order to form a correct estimate of this, it is necessary to take account of the number of refusals of admission, as well as of the actual admissions. This is illustrated by statistics for the year 1858, prepared for the Board of Lunacy in January last, which show that about as many patients were refused admission, from want of accommodation, as were actually admitted. Or, to be more precise, by giving the actual figures: while there were applications for admission on behalf of 151 patients, only 77 of the said patients, or rather more than one-half, were admitted, while 74 were refused admission from want of room. This unusual pressure was entirely in regard to *pauper* patients, and was undoubtedly solely or

Admissions.

Refusal of Applications for Admission.

Demand for Accommodation of Pauper Patients.

mainly due to the operation of the Lunatic Asylums (Scotland) Act passed two years ago. During the first half of the present year this pressure has materially diminished, in consequence, apparently, to a certain extent, at least, of the operation of a subsequent and supplementary Act,* which throws open various Poorhouses for the reception of pauper patients. This Act has been rendered necessary by the present inadequate provision for the proper accommodation of the insane poor of Scotland: but its operation is intended to be only temporary—until 1st January, 1863—that is until the various District Asylums of Scotland are open for the reception of patients. Indeed, till the latter event occurs the number of applications for admission on behalf of pauper patients is likely considerably to exceed the capabilities of the Institution to admit them. It has only been by temporarily fitting up as dormitories and otherwise apartments in, and departments of, the Institution originally intended for other purposes that it has been possible to accommodate the unusually large population of the past year. The female admissions preponderated over the males in the proportion of 42 to 37. The age of the greatest number of patients admitted was between 40 and 50: but there were nearly twice as many below the age of 40 as above that of 50. The single were to the married nearly as two to one. In no less than 11 cases the duration of insanity prior to admission was about or less than a week; in 27 it was less than a month; and in 47 less than six months. So that, in more than half the whole cases admitted, the duration of the disease did not exceed a few weeks or months. This is another most gratifying indication, added to the many we have adduced or given in former Annual Reports, of the fact that insane patients are now placed under treatment at a much earlier period in the progress of the disease than formerly. The good effects of this humane and enlightened conduct on the part of relatives and guardians is not hypothetical: as a practical illustration of the benefits that have already accrued, we would only refer to our remarks under the head of Recoveries. 6 patients were re-admitted for the second time and 6 for the third time: the intervals of recurrence or relapse varying in these cases from one month to thirty years. The occasional length of this interval is calculated to inspire with hope those who believe that one attack of insanity, even though it

Operation of Lunacy Acts of 1857 and 1858.

Temporary Accommodation of Pauper Patients.

Age, &c. of Patients Admitted.

Early periods of Admission.

Relapses or Re-admissions.

* Act 21 and 22 Vict. Cap. 89, "To amend an Act of the last Session for the Regulation of the Care and Treatment of Lunatics," &c. August, 1858.

terminate in recovery, must of necessity lead to another at no distant period of time. The interval is sometimes so great, that a long, useful, and happy life intervenes between the first and second attacks. In 29 cases no cause for the insanity was assigned or known; in 1 case the disease was attributed to excitement connected with the celebration of the Burns' Centenary; in the remaining cases the causes stated in the admission-schedules are not such as to call for special remark. In 46 cases there was no appreciable co-existent physical disease; in none of the remainder was the complication sufficiently important or novel to be noteworthy.

Intervals of Relapse.

It will sometimes be found that different districts of the same country are distinguished by particular forms of insanity. One Asylum will be found to have regularly a greater number of cases affected with a certain form of insanity than another. For instance, there are great differences in regard to cases arising from intemperance, which seem more prevalent near large towns—as Glasgow and Edinburgh—than in country districts such as ours. We have always had comparatively few cases of Dipsomania, or of insanity arising from intemperance; and patients of this class who have found their way hither have been chiefly the inhabitants of our large towns. Were we required to name the predominating character of the cases that present themselves for admission into this Asylum, we should indicate Melancholia, or insanity marked generally by despondency, and associated with suicidal propensity. We are not prepared to assign any distinct or appreciable cause for this. Some whole countries are characterised by this prevalent character of the insanity in their population. Such would appear to be the case in Norway, where the cause is supposed to be found in the solitary lives of the inhabitants, who are thinly scattered over the deep, gloomy valleys that intersect the various mountain ranges or fjelds. Of 79 admissions in this Asylum during the past year, 24 were cases of Melancholia, the females affected being twice as numerous as the males. The next most prevalent form of the disease in the patients admitted was Monomania—in 19 cases—this form of insanity being, like the preceding, frequently associated with suicidal tendency. Next in order stood Acute Mania—in 17 cases—while Dementia followed in 10. The number of cases of Chronic Dementia—of confirmed fatuity—was unusually large, in consequence of our having admitted several patients—natives of Perthshire—who had been discharged from other

Forms of Insanity characterising districts of Country.

Suicidal Melancholia a prevalent type of Insanity in Perthshire.

In Norway.

Chronic Dementia.

Asylums, to make room for the paupers of the counties or districts in which these Asylums are situated, in terms of arrangements with the District Boards of Lunacy. The majority of the patients so admitted were males: in 2 of them the disease was congenital; in 3 its duration had been between 30 and 40 years; in 7 upwards of 20 years; and in 10 upwards of 10 years. Suicidal or homicidal propensities, or both, are distinctly stated or avowed in 24 cases; but there is reason to believe they existed, at some period in the history of the disease, in a considerably larger proportion of cases. In a large number of the cases, in which a suicidal propensity is developed, the melancholia or despondency exhibits itself mainly in connection with the religious feelings. This peculiar and prevalent form of melancholia is frequently most difficult to eradicate or conquer, and, from its inveteracy, it is the forerunner often of incurable insanity.

Suicidal and Homicidal propensities

Religious Melancholia

We have almost yearly occasion to animadvert upon the deplorable condition, as to physical complications and as to bodily restraint, in which patients are occasionally brought to us. In some cases the condition in question has resulted from direct and deliberate maltreatment prior to admission; in others to culpable neglect of treatment; and in a third class of cases it would appear to be, in some measure, at least, unavoidable and beyond control. The present year forms no exception unfortunately, though instances of the kind immediately to be narrated are undoubtedly rare, and are becoming more and more so every day. One patient—a male—when admitted, had his hands fastened behind his back by an iron manacle, and his ankles were bound together by strong cords. When he was relieved of all his cords and manacles, he exhibited the most abject terror of the Asylum attendants, evidently fearful lest some still more refined cruelty were in store for him. And it was some days before his terror or mistrust gave place to a confidence, which thereafter increased daily up to the period of his decease. Freedom from all restraint, bathing, good diet, kind nursing, and the occasional visits of sympathising relatives, produced a rapid change for the better in his disposition and disease, and when he died subsequently, he showed himself to be full of gratitude for the benefits which he derived from his residence in the Institution. Careful examination, subsequent to admission, revealed in this unfortunate patient the following diseased conditions:—acute pleurisy, with bronchitis, on both sides of the chest; acute synovitis of both knee joints;

Deplorable condition in which Patients occasionally are Admitted.

Use of Restraint in Country Districts.

Illustrations of self-inflicted Injuries or Diseases.

fracture of the tenth ribs on both sides of the chest; and severe bruises of the scalp, which subsequently became abscesses. Synovitis was followed by suppuration in the interior of the right knee joint, and had the patient survived, and the state of his general system subsequently permitted such a step, amputation of the limb would probably have become necessary. In connection with this disease of the joint, diffuse abscesses in the thigh appeared; there were also enormous diffuse abscesses up the back connected with the fractured ribs, while large gangrenous bed sores completed the catalogue of diseases, attended with profuse wasting discharges, which gradually sapped his strength. He came to us emaciated to an extreme degree. Though he rallied for a time, hectic gradually supervened. He recovered completely *quoad* his attack of acute mania, but he died the victim of the serious physical diseases under which he suffered. The necroscopic examination discovered the following pathological conditions:—old pleuritic adhesions, generally distributed, but most abundant posteriorly and inferiorly—that is, opposite the fractured ribs; greater part of left lung and upper portion of right lung infiltrated with, and solidified by, grey miliary tubercle; lower lobe of right lung gangrenous opposite the fracture of the tenth rib; tenth ribs on both sides carious at or near their angles; large chronic abscesses on both sides of spine, extending down and underneath the skin of the back, external to, and not communicating with, the pleura, lined by or enclosed in a thick false membrane, opening on the back by numerous sinuses, which had discharged large quantities of sanious pus during the latter part of the patient's life; right knee joint entirely disorganized, bones soft and carious; left contained serous effusion, and its interior communicated with a large diffuse abscess in the thigh. In such cases as that above recited, the *primâ facie* evidence would lead to the suspicion of harsh or cruel treatment on the part of those charged with the care and conveyance of the patient prior to his admission into the Asylum. But we purposely give the above case as an illustration that it is necessary, in all such cases, to exercise a due amount of caution in coming to a judgment, or arriving at a conclusion, as to whether and where blame is attributable. The reputation—the interests of most estimable men—of most useful public servants, may be inadvertently sacrificed by an erroneous judgment or decision, based on insufficient evidence. Let us advert briefly to this patient's antecedents. He was labouring under

Caution r cessary ir accusatio of mal-tr ment.

acute mania. Before proper assistance was asked for, or at all events secured, he was permitted to tumble about on his head on the public causeway, to knock himself violently against bed-posts, or to push his hands or feet through the panels of doors, and to beat his chest most severely with both his fists. He appeared at the time to be insensible to all bodily pain, but his self-inflicted injuries produced the frightful fruits above recorded. At this stage in the history of the case, little or nothing appears to have been done to protect or prevent the poor patient from injuring himself; but immediately before he was brought to this Institution assistance was called in, restraint appears to have been at once applied as the only means for the patient's safety, and the form selected was to bind him down by 4 iron bars or posts driven into the floor of his room. There was not at this, nor at any subsequent time, any intentional or unnecessary harsh treatment on the part of his attendants, according to the testimony of his wife, who on the contrary certified to his having been very tenderly dealt with. The very few comments or remarks which we have to make on this painful case must not be regarded as an endeavour to account for the injuries or diseases described, or as a defence of the conduct of those charged with the care and conveyance of the patient prior to his reception here; even did we feel inclined, our data are too limited to enable us to do so. Still less must these remarks be considered as apologetic of the maltreatment, or neglect of treatment, of our Insane Poor. But we feel strongly —and we know abundantly that many a false accusation is brought against those charged with the management of the insane. We can see neither justice nor humanity in sacrificing the sane for the insane, as is not unfrequently done when an innocent attendant, for instance, is accused of having inflicted injuries which the patient himself has inflicted, and which could not have been reasonably avoided.

avoid- e acci- ts to the ane.

Accidents are constantly occurring in the best regulated Asylums in all countries, from causes which no human foresight can prevent or control, even in the presence of the most kind, experienced, and watchful attendants, and in the midst of all approved appliances for the comfort, cure, or safety of their inmates. When accidents cannot be altogether prevented within Asylums, it need not surprise us that they will occur occasionally in remote country districts, especially when ignorance prevails as to the modern treatment of the insane. The public is startled when it hears occasionally of a suicide in an Asylum; but did it consider the immense number of determined suicides admitted as patients, the duration of the propensity, the perseverance with which the object is attempted to be gained, and the ingenuity and variety of the means employed to effect their purpose, the sane public would be surprised, not that one suicide occurs now and then, but that so very few occur. Too little allowance is made, we fear, for the difficulties which Inspectors of Poor and their Subordinates or Assistants have to encounter in the management of cases in which immediate danger is threatened to the life or property of the patient, his friends, or the public, or where serious accidents have already occurred, and when, moreover, they must act at once and on their own responsibility and information. We are not of those who believe that physical restraint is *never* necessary in the treatment of insanity, nor in the management of the insane, and that it should not, *under any circumstances*, be had recourse to. And we hold it to be an evidence of gross bigotry and of great ignorance, as well as a piece of the most flagrant cruelty and injustice, to condemn a man merely because, conscientiously following out his sincere and honest convictions, and guided by the dictates of the purest and most disinterested humanity, he ventures to apply physical restraint in the few exceptional cases in which it is undoubtedly occasionally required in every Asylum. We cannot but regard it as somewhat inconsistent and anomalous in a Government, which charges itself with the "Regulation of the care and treatment of Lunatics," to punish most severely cases of maltreatment on the part of those charged with the management of insane paupers in country districts, without on the other hand previously educating them in what proper treatment consists. It appears to us a most legitimate duty for a Government Board of Lunacy to diffuse broadcast over the land—by means of lectures, printed circulars, advertisements in the public newspapers, or otherwise—sound information, not only as to the best management of insane patients from the time of the incursion of the disease to the date of their admission into an Asylum, but as to the nature and treatment of insanity generally. Were such information liberally diffused, there would be no excuse for ignorance, inhumanity, or maltreatment; and it would not then be—what in a measure or sense it is at present—an injustice to punish for improper treatment or management, some persons who may know of insanity and its treatment only by tradition, and who are ignorant of the features of the moral system of treatment, and of the

Difficulties of Inspectors of Poor &c. in the management of Insane Patients in Country Districts.

Use and abuse of physical restraint.

Diffusion of Information as to proper management of Insane.

modern management of Asylums for the insane. Evidences of such ignorance have occasionally "cropped out" during the past year in the form of requests for the loan, as patterns, of strait waistcoats or jackets—articles of restraint or appliances which are now banished from all properly regulated Asylums.

ejudices
l igno-
ice in
untry
stricts.

coveries.

lation to
ly period
treatment

The recoveries are 12 in excess of those of last year—a result, doubtless, attributable in a great measure, at least, to the comparatively early period in the progress of the disease when the patients were admitted under treatment. We have elsewhere and already stated, that 11 of the patients admitted had been insane less than a week, 27 less than a month, and 47 less than 6 months; or, in other words, in more than half of the admissions the duration of the disease had not exceeded 6 months. The patients who recovered were chiefly between the ages of 30 and 40; but, while there were 10 under 30, there were 14 above 40.

ustrations
results of
emature
noval.

ability to
tain dan-
ous Pa-
nts.

ecautions
cessary in
noval of
ngerous
tients.

We are again unfortunately in the painful position of being able to illustrate the evil effects of premature removal by a suicide, which occurred in a neighbouring village sometime ago. It was in the case of a woman, who was removed by her husband in direct opposition to our advice and cautions repeatedly tendered to him. When such accidents occur, relatives and the public are extremely apt to blame the Medical Superintendent for having discharged the unfortunate patient, or for having permitted his or her removal. In the case of a private patient, placed in the Asylum at the instance of relatives or guardians, who defray all necessary expenses of board, we are unfortunately powerless compulsorily to detain him until we are satisfied of his fitness again to be at large, should such relatives or guardians determine on his removal. All that we can do is, to point out the evils of premature removal and to suggest delay—enforcing our arguments by instances such as the suicide above alluded to. When, however, they continue obdurate, and refuse to listen to our advice or suggestions, or to be guided by the sad experience of others who have pursued and regretted a similarly foolish and perverse course of conduct, we are in the habit of exacting from the obligants for the board, or other responsible parties, a written document purporting that they have deliberately resolved on the removal of the patient on a given date, notwithstanding the repeated and distinctly understood assurances given by the Medical Superintendent, that, in his opinion, the said patient is not recovered nor in a fit state for removal. This we have found it absolutely necessary to do, to

base of the brain. In one case—that of a male aged 76—this was associated with a similar condition of the thoracic and abdominal aorta. The substance of the brain is noted as generally either normal or firm: only in one case—one of simple apoplexy in a woman of 72—was its substance at all easily lacerable. In 5 cases the cerebral substance was pale or anæmic—a result that may have arisen from post mortem changes or conditions, such as the posture of the body; in one case of Dementia in a male aged 59, the brain was somewhat atrophied. It is noteworthy, that 3 of the deaths—in which no special pathological conditions of the brain were apparent—arose in that form of insanity usually denominated General Paralysis. We have never met with "ramollissement," or other marked lesion of the brain in this affection; on the contrary, in the great majority of such cases, the brain has appeared to be quite normal in its characters. The experience of the past year still further strengthens us in the conviction that the term *General Paralysis* is a mischievous and unscientific one—a name used conveniently, it may be, but also ignorantly, to include a host of dissimilar affections; as such, it ought to be abolished from Psychological nomenclature. We have for several years entertained views on the nature and pathology of General Paralysis opposed to those currently received both by alienistes and medical men generally; and we are glad to find that the opinions of various alienistes, both British and Foreign, are gradually coming to our support. We have little doubt, that a very few years will suffice to alter materially current ideas regarding the forms or phases of insanity, presently included under the much-misused term—General Paralysis. Nor is this the only term or name in the current nomenclature of insanity or classification of mental diseases to which we object. The current division into Mania, Monomania, Melancholia, Dementia, and Amentia, is far, in our estimation, from being a scientifically correct or satisfactory classification. But it is necessary, for the sake of brevity in arrangement, to make use of some classification, and experience has proved the above to be the most simple, concise, and convenient one; and, as such only we adopt it in our statistical tables. Monomania we regard as a misnomer; and it is by no means unusual to find the same case of Insanity, at different stages of its progress, presenting the characters successively of Mania, Melancholia, and Dementia. We constantly experience the greatest difficulty in classifying cases under the heads above given: because, in reality, these

Cerebral Pathology.

Pathology of General Paralysis.

Absurdity of the term "General Paralysis."

Unsatisfactory Classification of Mental Diseases.

Necessity of a new nomenclature and classification.

heads or names do not indicate separate and well marked forms of insanity, but merely the symptoms, features, or phases which are for the time predominant. We desiderate a nosology or classification, which shall be at the same time practically useful and scientifically accurate; but this is neither the time nor place to offer suggestions or criticisms on the subject. Much has been said of late years of a change of type during the last half-century in fevers, inflammations, and other diseases, which are now of a much less sthenic or healthy character than formerly. Nor do we see any valid reason for doubting the fact, or for denying or setting aside the evidence which has been brought forward in proof thereof. But we are equally satisfied, though there is a lack of statistical proof, that there has been a corresponding alteration in the type of nervous affections generally, which have become likewise more typhoid or asthenic. This would appear to be due to the greater sensitiveness and delicacy of the cerebro-nervous organization, and its consequent greater susceptibility to disturbing influences. Such a condition of the cerebro-nervous system, again, would appear to be the heritage of our gradually advancing civilization, or, at least, of its concomitants.

Change of type in cerebral and nervous diseases.

Causes of such Change.

One of the many difficult subjects on which we have been consulted during the year has been the expectancy of life in certain classes of the insane. This subject has been brought under our notice more especially in connection with Life Insurance. In cases of annuities, for instance, to be purchased, or already existing, on the life of an insane person, relatives or Insurance Companies are frequently greatly interested pecuniarily in the probable tenure of life in the annuitant. A consideration of the subject in its practical bearings—a scrutiny of Psychological literature—and a correspondence with some of the first Psychological authorities in Britain—have led us to be surprised at the very little that is known, or that can be said, on so important a question. There is great meagreness of statistical information. We can do nothing to supply this deficiency further than by stimulating to the collection of materials by showing their present paucity. We cannot help expressing our regret that Government Boards or Bodies—[we speak generally, and do not refer specially to Scotland]—which alone are the recipients of statistics regarding the insane of every class in every part of the country, do not make it their business to collect materials, which may serve to elucidate obscure points in the natural history of insanity. However imbued with a desire, *individuals* have not the same facilities

Expectancy of life in the Insane in relation to Life-Insurance, &c.

Importance of collection and elaboration of Statistics.

utics of overnment oards the collec-on and dis-mination information.

for doing this; and a public which is burdened with the support of these generally most expensive bodies, has a right to exact a *quid pro quo* in the form of something more than a mere enumeration of inspections made and abuses exposed to view. The collection of such statistics, and more especially the deduction of general laws or conclusions from the mass of data, would doubtless prove of great interest to the nation. We would simply point to the labours of Dr. Farre in London as an illustration of the valuable results that may be expected from the elaboration of statistics in the hands of scientific departments of Government. It must not be supposed that we accuse the members of Government Boards of neglect, or that we attribute blame in any manner or degree. In all probability the individuals composing these Boards have their hands full enough with the stricter duties of their commissions; still it is a pity that they do not possess the requisite leisure and means for doing other than mere statute duties. From the inquiries we have instituted, we have reason to believe that popular as well as professional errors exist to some extent as to the duration or probabilities of life in the insane. In particular, the insane are too much regarded as a class characterised by greatly inferior chances of life compared with the sane: they are too little regarded as separable into classes, each of which is, within certain limits, or to a certain extent, characterised by a different chance or expectancy of life. It is popularly believed that insanity *per se* greatly shortens life; and, in certain of its forms or phases, undoubtedly it does. Disordered functional action of the brain, if intense, may kill speedily by exhaustion; hence many cases of acute mania terminate directly and rapidly in fatal asthenia. The propensity to suicide and to self-starvation in certain forms of insanity, and its complications with epilepsy or other incurable physical diseases, also account, in some measure, for the greater relative mortality among the insane than the sane. As a general rule, insanity is associated with a low tone of vitality, and this again renders the body more prone than usual to a great variety of morbid conditions, which materially tend to shorten life. But in certain forms or phases of the disease—for instance, in confirmed Dementia—life is frequently not at all shortened, or, at least, not to the extent that is generally supposed. Among the inmates of every Asylum are many persons who live to a ripe old age: they are surrounded by circumstances favourable to longevity; they are doomed to none of the toils and troubles of life; their home is quiet and peace-

[Side notes: "rrors as to chances of life in the insane." — "Chances of life in the different forms of insanity." — "Comparative longevity in chronic Dementia."]

ful; their exercise and diet regular; and they are frequently the very pictures of robust physical health. A table appended to our obituary statistics for the present year shows, that of 222 deaths since 1827, nearly one-half, or 46·39 per cent, occurred in persons over 50 years of age. Of 103 deaths in patients above the age of 50, 48 occurred between 50 and 60; 27 between 60 and 70; 21 between 70 and 80; and 7 between 80 and 90. The majority of deaths in each decennial period between 50 and 90 were cases of Dementia—of confirmed fatuity. Even in Dementia, the form of disease, and the age at which it supervenes, are important in regard to the prognosis. For instance, Senile Dementia may not necessarily, or at all, shorten life; it is part and parcel of the euthanasia; the brain, like all the other organs of the body, is becoming gradually weakened, and fatuity results. According to the first Report of the Board of Lunacy for Scotland [Appendix A, page 112] it would appear, that, of the whole *pauper* insane of Scotland, nearly 1-9th or 11·58 per cent, are above 60 years of age—a fact which argues strongly both in favour of their longevity and of their good treatment. There is probably still, as there has been for long, a vague popular idea that idiots never survive the age of 30. Recent statistics abundantly prove, however, that this statement is not altogether correct. In the valuable Report by the "Commissioners appointed by the Governor of Massachusetts to inquire into the condition of the idiots of the Commonwealth,"* it is stated, that of 574 idiots examined, 374 were over 25 years of age, and no less than 292 were capable of improvement in their physical and mental health. The majority of idiots are the subjects of a variety of abnormal cerebral and physical conditions; body and mind alike are imperfectly developed, and it is not surprising that their viability, or chances of life, should be considerably less than those of sane persons with normal or healthy physiques. But *quoad* the mere mental condition—or in other words, in simple idiocy, when the physical health is good—we believe the tenure of life to be much greater than in the bulk of ordinary idiots. Even in regard to some of the most fatal or incurable forms of insanity, we are of opinion that great errors have been committed in speculations on the probable duration of life. For instance, what is called "General Paralysis" has been usually described as certainly fatal in 2 or 3 years at farthest: but there is now no doubt that the duration of this disease is frequently much greater.

Comparative longevity of the Pauper insane.

Chances of life in idio[ts]

Chances of life in General Paralys[is]

* "On the Causes of Idiocy;" being a Supplement to said Report. Edinburgh, 1858: p. 55.

Occupation of Mansion-House and Grounds of Pitcullen Bank.

The occupation of the House and grounds of Pitcullen Bank has proved a material benefit to the Institution in a variety of ways. It has enabled us to multiply and vary the means of occupation and amusement among the patients. Without this we should have had great difficulty in providing for the comparatively large population of male patients able and willing to work a sufficient amount and variety of out-of-door employment. We have no hesitation in affirming our belief, that the value of the property of Pitcullen Bank is being daily increased by the labours of the pauper patients. The grounds were taken possession of in a state of the greatest disorder: the garden was overrun with weeds; flower borders were obliterated; walks were overgrown with grass; fences were out of repair; the walls in some places were giving way; many of the fruit-trees and fruit-bearing shrubs were worn out; and it seemed a task of some years to produce anything like order or beauty out of such a chaos. Separate groups of patients have, during the year, been engaged in trenching the grounds for potatoes and other vegetables—in pruning the fruit-trees—in trimming the hedges—in cutting grass—in pointing the walls—in repairing and painting wooden and iron work—in pumping water—and in keeping the flower-garden in a state of good order. The change produced by these labours has been very gratifying. The parks afford pasture for 3 cows; the offices are most useful as storehouses for potatoes, fruit, wood, garden implements, and as workshops, in both of which classes of conveniences the Asylum is otherwise very deficient. The grounds already yield no inconsiderable addition to the revenue of the Institution in the form of garden produce—kitchen vegetables and fruit; and there is every reason to expect that they will be still more productive than they are at present. The occupation of the lodge, at the entrance-gate, has been given to a married attendant as a reward of faithful service. Again, in summer especially, the Pitcullen grounds form a favourite resort for games of cricket, foot-ball, or bowls, as well as for reunions and fêtes of all kinds—and in which all classes of the inmates join—and, lastly, visits are paid by individual patients to the house of the Medical Superintendent—visits which tend to the formation and strengthening of pleasant social ties. In Pitcullen House or grounds the patients feel themselves, in a measure, free of restraint—they are beyond the Asylum walls, and they enjoy the change of scene as a valued privilege. Other Scotch and English Asylums have lately attached to their grounds mansion-houses

Margin notes: ...cupation Mansion-ouse and ...ounds of ...tcullen ...ank. — ...dvantages ...the institution. — ...ield and ...arden labour of ...atients. — ...ewards to ...aithful attendants. — ...mportance ...f adjunct ...stablishments.

and gardens similar to those of Pitcullen; and the principle of possessing adjunct establishments of a similar kind, either as suitable residences for the medical superintendents, or as private retreats for patients belonging to the higher ranks of society, is now fully acknowledged and recommended by the highest authorities on the management of Asylums in this country.

Occupation of patients.

A shoemaker has been added to our industrial staff; and under his superintendence a comparatively large amount of shoemaking has been done by 3 or 4 patients. Several patients have acted most acceptably as tailors. Others have been employed as masons, among the fruit of whose work may be enumerated the building of a range of pig-styes—

Mason-wor

the formation of new walks and walls beside the farm-buildings—and the repair of the walls of the grounds of the Asylum and Pitcullen. We were fortunate in having among the patients, for a time, 2 excel-

Cookery an confectionery.

lent bakers and cooks—one of either sex—who not only gave lessons in the arts of confectionery and cookery to various of the officers of the Institution and to their fellow-patients, but who supplied various entertainments with the produce of their skill.

Public acknowledgment of services of attendants.

A most gratifying public testimony was lately offered to the faithful and long services of the attendants of the Institution by the award of the first premium of the "Society for Improving the Condition of the Insane" to Mr. Adam Smith, who has been for the long period of 29 years a servant—and a most attached servant—of the Institution. This Society, whose headquarters are in London, annually offers for open competition to attendants on the insane throughout Great Britain and Ireland premiums for meritorious conduct and length of service. Another of our attendants has been attached to the service of the Asylum for 25 years. It is further gratifying to be able to state, that there seems to be a growing desire among artizans, labourers, plough-

Demand fo employmen as Asylum attendants.

men, and other eligible persons, to become employed as Asylum-attendants. At present we have 36 candidates for the first vacancy. We are in the habit, in consequence of the number of applications, of keeping a list of candidates, showing the nature of their qualifications and the character of their recommendations, from which list we select

List of applicants.

according to eligibility when vacancies occur. These applications are generally more numerous when, from any cause, there is a general dearth of work among the operative classes of the community; but the demand for employment in the Institution is, in a great measure, independent of such circumstances. Old soldiers are perhaps the most common applicants; next follow labourers and ploughmen; artizans present themselves less frequently, unfortunately, in consequence of their labour generally being in greater demand and their wages high in "good times." This class of applicants is, however, to us the most important, inasmuch as carpenters, masons, plumbers, shoemakers, tailors, blacksmiths, gasfitters, and gardeners are always useful in a large institution. We have also had applications from schoolmasters, mill-overseers, commercial travellers, and others, belonging to a higher rank in life than artizans or labourers, whom family misfortunes or other causes had compelled to seek such a means of subsistence. Though the majority of applicants for situations were actuated by the desire simply for an honest and honourable subsistence, there were some who professed their wish to devote themselves to what they believed to be a useful and important field of labour. We are in the habit of appointing no one, who has not been fully made aware beforehand of the serious and irksome nature of the duties which he proposes entering upon.

tizan at-
idants.

estimonies
favour of
lucational
nd recrea-
onal mea-
ires.

The strongest testimony that can be borne to the usefulness of the means which we have been for some years in the habit of employing, for the education and recreation of our patients, consists in the fact, that similar appliances for instruction and amusement have been established — to a minor degree—in some other Asylums; while many persons who, when these appliances were originally introduced, sneered at them as absurdities, or the fruits of youthful enthusiasm, now recognise them as important and solid advantages. Doubtless, in this, as in many other things, extremes are most dangerous. Education and recreation among the insane may be carried to excess—they may become the "hobbies" of superintendents—or they may not be made use of at all as auxiliary means of treatment. The one evil is probably as great as the other, and both are sedulously to be guarded against. *In medio tutissimus* is here, as everywhere, a safe principle of guidance, and we profess to do no more than attempt to strike the "happy medium." We are perfectly aware that a feeling exists—in England more especially — that in Asylums where amusement abounds work is found neglected—that those distinguished for balls and concerts, pic-nics and walking excursions, lectures and classes, are not those distinguished for well kept gardens—well cultivated fields—well filled workshops—or a full exchequer. This, however, is an idea as unjust as it is ungenerous;

Dangers of
xtreme
iews or
ractices.

Work and
relaxation
compatible
and neces-
sary.

the two things are quite compatible; occupation and relaxation alternate with, and assist, and do not antagonise, each other. We believe that misconceptions, where they exist, do so mainly in consequence of prejudiced or ignorant persons not having for themselves witnessed the working of the system which they condemn. Another mistake, which we would take the liberty of indicating to cavillers, is this, that the management of Asylums in one country is not of itself a safe guide to their management in another. The inner life and the details of management in the Asylums of England and Ireland differ in various particulars from those of Scotland, just as the customs of the English and Irish differ somewhat from those of the Scotch. The same system of management is found not to be equally suited for the Asylums of these three countries—so much so, that we have known English Superintendents objected to as candidates for the charge of Scotch Asylums on the ground of their very experience; and the contrast is still greater between British and Foreign Asylums. He, therefore, who thinks that the same unmodified system of management should prove suitable in Scotland which is found serviceable in England or Ireland, Germany or France, America or India, is simply guilty of unpardonable ignorance of human nature, whether in its healthy or diseased manifestations. For instance, as a general rule, no amusement is perhaps more extensively or more thoroughly enjoyed in the Scotch Asylums than dancing, while we have the testimony of several English Superintendents to the effect, that in many English County Asylums dancing would be the reverse of an amusement.

Differences in tastes, habits, &c. in the insane of different districts or countries.

Our Course of Lectures during the past winter has been both full and varied, as the following programme will testify:—

Winter course of lectures.

I. Programme of Lectures.

	Lecturer.	Subject.	Date.
1.	Rev. Arch. Russell, Newburgh.	Life of Sir Henry Havelock.	8th Nov. 1858.
2.	Hugh Barclay, LL.D. Sheriff-Substitute of Perthshire.	Words.	15th ,, ,,
3.	William Blair, Esq. Perth.	Photography; with Illustrations.	29th ,, ,,
4.	Alex. Smith, Esq. Secretary of the University of Edinburgh.	Chaucer and his Works.	24th Dec. ,,
5.	J. Cruickshank, Esq. Falkland.	What?	10th Jan. 1859.
	Dr. Lyell, Newburgh.	Why?	
6.	Rev. John Paton, Chaplain to	The Reformation.	18th ,, ,
7.	H.M. Indian Forces.		24th ,, ,,
8.	Rev. Alex. Wallace, Glasgow.	Peasant Literature of Scotland.	9th Feb. ,,
9.	Professor Blackie, University of Edinburgh.	Modern Greece and the Ionian Islands.	18th ,, ,,
10.	Thomas Miller, LL.D. Rector of the Perth Academy.	Optics; with Illustrations.	25th ,, ,,
11.	Andrew Murray, Esq. of Conland.	Structure and Habits of Insects; with Illustrations.	14th March, ,,
12.	Rev. R. J. Craig, Perth.	Animal Instinct and Intelligence.	11th April, ,,

urse of adings.

In order to vary the character of the lectures, a new feature has been introduced this year in the form of Readings from some of the most approved British and American poets and novelists. They were made most pleasantly to alternate with the lectures, and they have proved most useful and interesting, not less from their novelty than from their inherent excellence. We subjoin a programme, as a specimen of the kind of Readings selected.

II. Programme of Readings.

	Reader.	Subject.	Date.
1.	Rev. John Paton.	Selections from *Noctes Ambrosianæ.*	2d Nov. 1858.
2.	Dr. Lorimer.	Selections from *Mansie Waugh.*	22d ,, ,,
3.	Sheriff Barclay.	,, Stevens' *Lectures on Heads.*	6th Dec. ,,
4.	Rev. John Paton.	,, *Longfellow's Poems, &c.*	20th ,, ,,
5.	Miss Shearer. Rev. John Paton. Dr. Lorimer.	,, *Merchant of Venice.*	31st Jan. 1859.
6.	Dr. Lorimer.	*How I became a Yeoman.*	28th March, ,,

ening asses.

In addition to the Classes instituted in former years, during the past winter Mr. Schaefer of the Perth Academy conducted a Class for

German among a few of the higher ranks of patients, while Dr. Lorimer established one for the Elements of Music among the attendants.

III. Programme of Classes.

	Teacher.	Subject.	Pupils.	Date of Meeting.
1.	Mr. H. F. Schaefer, Perth Academy.	German.	Higher Class Patients.	Evenings of Friday.
2.	Dr. Lorimer.	Elements of Music.	Attendants.	Thursday.
3.	Miss Giddings.	Psalmody.	All classes of Patients and Attendants.	Thursday.
4.		Religious Instruction.	Do.	Sunday.
5.	Miss Shearer, and Mr. C——.	Reading, History, and Geography.	Pauper Patients.	Wednesday.
6.		Writing and Arithmetic		Saturday.

Amusements. Pic-nics.

The scenes of pic-nic excursions during the summers of 1858 and 1859 have been Plean, Stirling, and Bannockburn ; Murthly Castle and Birnam Hill, Dunkeld ; Crieff and Drummond Castle ; Dunsinnan Hill ; Glenalmond ; Kinfauns ; and Campsie Linn. Carriage drives, as heretofore, have chiefly taken the direction of Pitcaithly Wells and the Bridge of Earn ; Stormontfield Ponds ; Glencarse and Scone.

Athletic games. Cricket.

Athletic Games have come into greater favour than heretofore. A Cricket Club has been formed, and a uniform manufactured for its members by the ladies of our community. "Excelsior" has been chosen as the distinctive appellation of the club, and each member bears this "strange device" emblazoned on the front of his blue or scarlet bonnet. Last summer several cricket matches were played for cricket belts and other prizes.

Foot-ball.

Football has also become very popular ; and it is a game better suited than cricket or bowls for spring or autumn weather—still more so for that of winter.

Burns' Centenary Concert.

Burns' Centenary was celebrated by a concert of Scotch music, recitations of original verses in honour of the Bard or his works being interspersed among the musical performances. During the past year we have received a greater amount of assistance in our amusements *ab extra* than in previous years.

Professional assistance at concerts, &c.

It affords us much pleasure to avail ourselves of this opportunity of offering our most grateful acknowledgments to Sir Thomas Moncreiffe and Lord Charles Kerr for their kindness in placing at our command the services of the Band of the Royal Perthshire Militia on the occasion of our Christmas Ball ; to Mr. George Tedder, Professor of Music,

London, for his services at one of our concerts; to the Choir of the East Church, Perth, for a most delightful concert given by them in the Hall of the Institution; to the Bridgend Flute Band for their services on the occasion of our Queen's Birthday Fête; and though last, certainly not least, to various "Fair Maids" and wives of Perth, who have rendered most efficient and acceptable assistance at various of our concerts, balls, and other amusements. Select parties of patients, especially of the higher ranks, have been sent to town to be present at, to see or hear, Washington Friend's American Panorama; Wiljalba Frikell's Magic Entertainment; Pell's American Minstrels; Dr. Mark's Concert; Mr. Herbert's and Mrs. Baker's Concerts; the Highland Games; the Annual Races; the County and City Flower Shows; Public Lectures by Professor Blackie on "Education;" Professor Ferrier on the "Life and Genius of Burns;" Dr. Stirling on "Public Health;" Dr. Lindsay on "Substitutes for Paper Material;" and Mr. Montgomery on "Knowledge;" and various Curling Matches at Scone or elsewhere. Our reunions occasionally present features that are as pleasing as they are unexpected and novel. Not only do old patients, who, since they resided within our precincts, have done brave service in the battle of life, sometimes revisit their old associates on such occasions, but they are not seldom the scenes of the happy meetings of relatives. Wives, daughters, sisters, and other relatives, came from considerable distances to be present at our Christmas festivities, to meet "for auld langsyne," and, as it were, at their "ain fireside," those nearest and dearest to them. Such meetings and greetings of relatives have all the fervour and familiarity which they would have had in private homes; and the affections thus publicly displayed, and at such seasons, have had the happiest effects, not only on the individual patients visited, but on the body of the inmates at large. They feel that their position does not place them beyond the pale of society, does not exclude them from the enjoyment of the ordinary endearing relationships of life. By means of correspondence, moreover, which is freely permitted to certain of the inmates, associations of a harmless and pleasant kind are maintained with the external world. A gentleman lately gave a celebration party, at which his wife and another female relative, who came 50 miles for the purpose, were present. Nor is it uncommon for patients to visit their relatives if within a reasonable distance from Perth, spending the day with them or otherwise; in

Visits to amusements in town.

Reunions and evening parties: their family character.

Meetings of Patients with Relatives.

Visits to relatives at a distance.

other cases the relatives visit the patients here, accompanying them in drives or walks in the neighbourhood. Taking advantage of well-known feminine tastes and instincts, as developed in the young, and bearing in mind the similarity, in many respects, between insane persons and children, it occurred to us that the introduction of Dolls into the female galleries as playthings might be useful, if only as furnishing sources of amusement. The result proved the correctness of our conjecture. They were at once seized upon with the greatest eagerness by individual patients, who bestowed upon them names, and tended them with all the fondness of mothers, while the whole inmates of a gallery capable of doing so were set to work to contribute articles of dress. Some ladies take an intense and unceasing delight in fondling their dolls, which are their inseparable companions. But these playthings have conferred higher benefits, as may be illustrated by a recent case, in which a lady labouring under puerperal mania began to recover from the moment she cast eyes upon a doll, her recovery being speedy and satisfactory. Our Library, Museum, and Bazaar are daily receiving solid and valuable additions; they are now in full working order, and furnish sources of great pleasure and of much instruction to our inmates.

Dolls in th female galleries: their uses.

Library, Museum, and Bazaar

Had our late esteemed chaplain, the Rev. John Paton, now attached to H. M. Forces in India, been at his post to have presented his report to the Directors for the present year, he would probably have referred to an experiment, which was suggested by him and initiated under his auspices, in regard to the circulation of the Bible among certain classes of the patients. It is notorious that in some forms of insanity, marked by great exaltation or depression of the religious sentiments, the study of the Bible is calculated to foster the disease and to render nugatory all the efforts of the physician to eradicate it. It is equally well known that certain Books or parts of the Bible—such as the Book of Revelation—are usually selected for study by such patients, these parts or sections being the ones best calculated to inflame the passions or excite intensely the emotions. In such cases, or under such circumstances, it is usual to prevent all access to the Bible. But, undoubtedly, there is a serious responsibility attachable to shutting up the Bible from those whom certain other of its books or sections might tend to soothe and comfort. Hence it was supposed, that, if certain apparently harmless books, or parts of the Bible, could be bound separately and supplied in special cases, instead of the entire book, much

Circulation of the Bibl among cer tain classe of patients.

Isolation o certain Books or Gospels.

good might be achieved, while much evil might be avoided. Accordingly the experiment was begun with the book of Psalms and the Gospel of Luke, which were had separately at a very small price. It may be here mentioned that these and other separate books or portions of the Bible are kept for sale by various booksellers in Edinburgh and elsewhere; they are habitually used in some hospitals, public institutions, and schools; the printing is large and legible; the books occupy small bulk, and they are in many ways extremely convenient. Our experience is not yet so great as to enable us to give a final and decided opinion; but, so far as it goes, it is favourable to the accomplishment of the object originally contemplated.

Under the operation of the Lunatic Asylums (Scotland) Act, 1857, the Perthshire District Board of Lunacy has resolved on erecting a Pauper Asylum at or near Murthly, Dunkeld; and preliminary or ulterior steps have been taken in regard to the erection of Pauper Asylums by various other District Boards of Lunacy throughout Scotland. When these Asylums are ready for occupation, one effect will probably be, the removal from this Asylum of its whole *Pauper* population. A large

'he future f Murray's toyal Institution.

amount of space will thus be rendered available for other purposes, the disposal of which space the Directors of the Institution have for some time had under consideration. The Act of Parliament above alluded to confers great benefits on the *pauper* insane of Scotland; it compels the most ample and admirable provision for their housing, comfort, and cure; it places at their command all modern appliances for the treatment of their malady, which science or humanity can supply or suggest.

mportance f Asylums or the middle classes.

But it does not confer equivalent advantages upon insane persons above the rank of paupers; in some details it even treats them with injustice, though unwittingly no doubt, in evidence whereof we need only refer to the fact, that while (Section 31) 2s 6d is charged for the Sheriff's warrant in the case of the admission of a *Pauper* into an Asylum, 5s is charged in the case of every person "not being a Pauper," who is therefore generally denominated, in contradistinction, a *private* patient. Now, the distinction between a pauper and private patient is probably improperly or imperfectly understood. The charge for the maintenance of the first named falls on a Parochial Board, which is made up of more or less wealthy heritors; that for the latter falls on one or more relatives or friends frequently little able, from their scanty earnings, to afford such an expense. We are here contrasting, for reasons which will immediately become apparent, the pauper insane with other classes of the poor insane—that is, the insane belonging to the operative ranks of society, labourers, artizans, and the like—as well as with the insane of the middle ranks of society. In the case of the pauper, parochial relief is at once sought for, no feelings of delicacy or pride allow them-themselves to interfere with the request for assistance. In the case of a poor private patient, the patient himself, his relatives or guardians, scorn and scout the idea of becoming dependent on charitable aid so long as there remains to either of them a single penny. Vast sacrifices are frequently to our knowledge made to gather together the minimum board charged by a public or private Asylum ; hardships are endured at home to an incredible extent, in order that an insane husband or wife, mother or sister, son or daughter, as the case may be, may be tended and treated with care and comfort in an Asylum. Perhaps the sum is the result of a subscription among several families of artizans very ill able to spare any drain on their finances. In a word, the expense of board for a private patient of the operative class, and even of a rank much above this in social status, falls heavily on one or more individuals, to whom the loss or expenditure of a shilling may be matter of vital importance ; while, in the case of a pauper, it falls lightly on a body of ratepayers well able to afford it. Humanity would suggest that every assistance should be rendered to the relatives or guardians of a private patient in such a case ; but from their construction and mode of government few Asylums are in a position to do so. At present the "indigent private insane" of Scotland, to borrow the designation used by the Board of Lunacy for the classes of the insane we have been above contrasting with paupers, are associated mainly in public Asylums with paupers on the one hand and with patients of the affluent classes on the other. Under the operation of the Act of 1857, most of the existing Scotch Asylums will become virtually Pauper Asylums—that is, the bulk of their population will consist of paupers, while the contemplated new District Asylums are intended solely or virtually for paupers. The Board of Lunacy, however, in its first Report (page xii), favours the idea of associating, to a limited extent at least, the indigent private insane with paupers in the new District Asylums. To such association there are at present legal difficulties ; but there are many stronger reasons why, in many, if not in most or all, cases, it is preferable to keep the pauper insane as a class by themselves, and to associate the

Burden of insanity on the operative and middle classes.

Association of Private and Pauper Insane.

indigent and affluent private insane in establishments devoted to them alone. Insanity is a more grievous burden perhaps on individuals belonging to the middle ranks than to any other grade or class of society either above or below them, for those above them in status can afford to command all the luxuries of life, the best medical treatment, and every necessary appliance for their comfort and cure ; while paupers at once throw themselves on parochial relief, and are amply cared for under the provisions of the Act of 1857. Let us, however, suppose a professional man of good status, but of limited income—a large family as well as himself depending on his daily exertions for support—becoming insane, no uncommon event in this age of eager competition. His source of income at once fails ; his family are suddenly reduced to penury ; his other relatives or friends belong perhaps to a lower rank in society than himself, and are possessed of but little of this world's goods. In such circumstances, it is matter of extreme difficulty, perhaps impossibility, to raise an annual sum of £50 or upwards, which is necessary to secure in an Asylum anything like the comfort or the society to which he has been accustomed. Or let us suppose the case of a poor governess becoming insane from the intense exertions she is called upon to make for a livelihood, or from the vicissitudes of her hard lot. She has moved in good circles of society in former times; she is most accomplished, amiable, and intelligent ; she has lost her parents, and has been cast an orphan on the wide, cold world, unprovided for ; friends she has none ; she is struggling for a bare subsistence ; and when insanity smites her to the dust, her employers are unwilling to burden themselves with her maintenance. In either of the cases above sketched, relatives or friends may be willing or able to pay a rate of board considerably below that charged for a pauper ; if not, the only other resource is to cast the unfortunate patients on the poor roll. Now, whether such patients are admitted as paupers, or as "indigent private insane," in our opinion they ought to be treated in their calamity as gentlemen and ladies, as educated, well-bred persons, accustomed to all the comforts and conventionalities of good society ; they should associate in the Asylum with the same rank of society in which they were accustomed to move out of it. Unless in Asylums specially devoted to private, as contradistinguished from pauper, patients, or under such arrangements as have for years been carried out in this Asylum—whereby, under special circumstances, the Directors have placed the advantages of the best accommodation, the best society, and the highest comforts at the command of those who have formerly moved in good circles of society, irrespective of the rates of board their relatives or guardians are now able to afford—such a professional man and governess while insane must become in all essential particulars paupers, they must be inmates of a Pauper Asylum, walk in pauper galleries, sleep in pauper dormitories, and live on pauper fare. But in certain other respects they are infinitely worse off than paupers proper. Pauper fare and pauper clothing, pauper bedding and pauper housing, pauper occupations and pauper enjoyments, are all in themselves good *quoad* the class paupers (we speak of the arrangements which already exist in the Scotch Public Asylums, and of those which are likely to exist in the new District Asylums), and apart from the associations which they call forth, or are calculated to call forth, are not necessarily objectionable to, nor unfitted for, the insane of ranks in society above the pauper class. But sensitive, educated minds, unless sunk hopelessly in fatuity, naturally shrink from association with a class upon which they have always, rightly or wrongly, looked down as inferior to themselves in birth and breeding. The mixed character of the population in many public Asylums, and in particular the association under the same roof, or within the same grounds, of pauper patients, with inmates belonging to the higher ranks, are probably strong reasons why hitherto private patients have been very much treated in private Asylums, especially in England. There is, however, in many quarters, and on divers accounts, a prejudice against private boarding-houses or retreats—Asylums they may be called, but they are seldom entitled to the appellation of hospitals for the treatment of insanity, which all Asylums undoubtedly should be; such establishments, from lack of the necessary capital and the absence of public patronage and supervision, cannot, and do not, possess the same advantages for treatment as public Asylums. Indeed, there are many and cogent reasons for preferring large public Asylums to small private boarding-houses, for certain classes at least of the insane of the middle and higher ranks. The strong prevalent feeling against private houses is one daily met with in our experience, and in that of every superintendent of an Asylum. We constantly see cases, where, in order to prevent Parochial Boards sending pauper patients to the cheapest private boarding-houses, the relatives implement—at great personal sacrifices—the difference of board between our charges and those of the

Private *versus* Public Asylums:

boarding-houses in question, in order that the patient in whom they are interested may get what they conceive to be the superior benefits of treatment in a public Asylum, which is, as it were, under the management and supervision of the public, whose Directors and officers are well known, and in whom they have every confidence. But we purposely here avoid discussing in full the advantages and disadvantages of associating the pauper and private insane; the respective benefits of public and private Asylums; or the superior merits of treatment in Asylums over treatment at home. We have done this on previous occasions, and we cannot here revert to the subject. The want of public Asylums for private patients, that is, insane persons not paupers, especially belonging to the middle classes of society, has been long and much felt in England, where two institutions have been erected within the last few years mainly to meet this want—viz. those of Coton Hill near Stafford, and Cheadle near Manchester. And very recently, the urgent necessity for farther establishments of the same kind has been fully pointed out by the Earl of Shaftesbury, Dr. Harvey of Southampton, and others. In Scotland, there is no such institution quite apart from a Pauper Asylum. That it is already much required, and that it will be still more urgently wanted when the new District Asylums are built, we are firmly convinced.

Want of an Asylum for the middle classes in Scotland.

With a view to meet this clamant public want, the Directors of Murray's Royal Institution have it in view, under the new circumstances created by the operation of the Act of 1857, and which have been above more fully alluded to, to devote it mainly to the reception of private patients—that is, in general terms, patients not paupers. The accommodation left vacant by the removal of our pauper population will probably be remodelled and adapted mainly for patients—1. Of the highest ranks in society; 2. Of the middle classes; and 3. Of the operative classes, who decline, or are independent of, parochial relief. This proposed alteration in the constitution of this Asylum is adverted to by the Board of Lunacy in their first annual report in the following terms (p. xxiii) :—"The Directors of that Establishment have resolved that it shall continue to fulfil its original purpose of being a 'public institution for charitable purposes;' and as they consider that this purpose would not be fulfilled by the reception of paupers maintained by parochial rates, they have determined to reserve their Asylum for the accommodation of private indigent insane, and of patients belonging to the higher classes." The Directors of this Asylum have always acted

Murray's Royal Institution to become an Asylum for the middle and higher classes.

under the belief that they were doing a greater amount of real good to individuals, as well as conferring a greater benefit on society at large, in assisting the generous and self-sacrificing efforts of relatives and guardians, in indigent private cases, by reducing the rates of board, or otherwise, and in reserving their accommodation for patients of the middle and higher classes, than in devoting the Institution under their charge to the purposes solely or mainly of a Pauper Asylum. They have considered themselves privileged—from the nature of their Royal Charter and organization—by having it in their power to benefit the classes indicated; and so satisfied have they been of the soundness of the principle, and of the benefits of the practice in question, that they are glad the Act of 1857 opens up to them an opportunity of extending their efforts in the same direction. So far as we are aware, when the contemplated alteration is carried out, Murray's Royal Institution will be the only Public Asylum in Scotland unassociated with, and apart from, a Pauper Asylum or department, which devotes itself chiefly to patients of the middle and higher classes. Hence it cannot fail to offer peculiar advantages in the eyes of those who object to permit insane relatives to associate with the uneducated or degraded—with paupers; who are prejudiced against private Asylums, or who from any cause prefer public to private establishments for the treatment of insanity; and who have more confidence in Asylum, than in home, treatment. We must be excused, for obvious reasons, from making any remarks on the special qualifications of this Asylum as an hospital or residence for patients of the higher and middle ranks. The Royal Commissioners of 1855, however, in their Report (dated 1857, page 98) refer to its capabilities "of the highest order," and go on to remark: "The establishment consists of a well constructed building, specially designed for the treatment of the insane, an adjoining mansion and pleasure grounds, and also a farm house and farm buildings. The whole are well placed on a large estate in a picturesque and retired situation, easily accessible by railway, and within a short distance of a large town. It is evident, that, in these respects, the Institution possesses a valuable combination of advantages *equal if not superior to any similar establishment in the United Kingdom.*"

Capabilities and Advantages of Murray's Royal Institution.

We have been repeatedly applied to for suggestions or advice regarding the best construction or arrangement of Asylums. There are very many points on which we should gladly avail ourselves of an opportunity of expressing our opinions; and the present is certainly a

Suggestions for the Construction and Organization of Asylums.

favourable time, when the various District Boards of Lunacy throughout Scotland are making arrangements for the erection of new Pauper Asylums. But we cannot do more here than offer a few remarks on certain points, which appear to us of special importance to all who are concerned in the erection of our new District Asylums. Hitherto, in the construction of Asylums, it has been unfortunately too customary altogether, or in great measure, to ignore the experience and opinions of Psychologists—of men versant with the requirements of the insane—of those who have had the charge of hospitals for the treatment of insanity. These professional men ought to know better, and we confidently assert they do know better, than any other authorities whatever, how Asylums should be best constructed and regulated with a view to their use as curative establishments. But architects alone have been consulted, and have been allowed to manage all the details of construction, from the plans upwards, unguided by the assistance of the opinion of medical experts. The results have been sufficiently appalling, in all countries, to prevent a repetition of such experiments or such procedure. In older Asylums throughout Europe, irremediable errors in construction are attributable to architects; vast amounts of money have been squandered on buildings not at all adapted, or very ill adapted, to the purposes for which they were, or at least should have been, intended; classification and proper treatment have been rendered impossible, and the defects have been such that no labour on the part of the medical superintendents could correct or supply them. We have ourselves in Ireland seen new Asylums, or portions thereof, belonging to and erected by Government—London architects being employed, and no medical men having been consulted—so utterly unfit for their intended purposes, that before they could be inhabited or occupied, it was necessary to pull them down and rebuild them, or to make radical and most expensive alterations. In some of these Asylums—the only principle evident in the construction whereof seemed to be a sordid and ill-timed economy—we have seen unplastered walls—ventilation a myth—and heating anything but a boon to the miserable inmates. This would appear to be a result of Government routine and red-tapeism; but it is a disgrace to the age that such a state of matters should exist, and we confidently hope the time has arrived in Scotland when it shall no longer be permitted to exist. Most of the existing, or at least older, Scotch Asylums are specimens of faulty construction, for which architects alone

[Margin notes: ecessity of Medical uperintendence *ab itio.* — rrors of rchitects.]

are to blame; they are the very reverse of models upon which to construct our new District Asylums. There is every reason to believe that many, if not all, of the District Asylums will be constructed on proper principles; and we fondly hope that these institutions will furnish models for pauper Asylums, which other countries will see it their interest to imitate. Not only are medical experts being consulted in regard to the sites and construction of such District Asylums as have been already determined upon, but in some cases at least the Medical Superintendent is being appointed as the first, and most important, step, in the organization of the establishment or construction of the building. His duty is to direct the architect in his plans, to superintend the building operations, and to visit the Asylums of this and other countries, with a view to bring the united experience of Europe, and it may be America, to bear upon the rendering the particular establishment under his charge as perfect in its appointments as it is possible to make it. We have no hesitation in affirming that such appointments are correct in principle, and we trust they will be found equally economical in practice. The Members of the Inverness District Board of Lunacy have set a noble example by appointing a medical superintendent before even the plans of their Asylum have been decided upon; it is intended that he should reside on the site of the proposed Asylum and personally superintend the works *ab initio*. We sincerely trust that this example will be followed forthwith by other District Boards of Lunacy, being well assured they will ultimately find it to their advantage to do so. Architects of eminence in England, as well as Scotland, have been invited to send in competition plans for certain of the new District Asylums, and some of these architects at least are sedulously availing themselves of the opportunity of gathering the ideas of the leading medical superintendents throughout the country regarding the best construction of hospitals for the insane. Besides, architects have an admirable guide in the rules laid down anent the construction of Asylums in the first Report of the Board of Lunacy (Page 115, Appendix C). And, lastly, the fact that all plans selected by District Boards must be submitted to, and approved of by, the General Board of Lunacy at Edinburgh before being put into the hands of the builder, yields an additional security that the forthcoming District Asylums of Scotland will be a credit to the country, in so far as they will be wanting in no essential requirement for the comfort and cure of the insane poor.

Principles on which new Dist[rict] Asylums should be Erected.

Appointment of Medical Superinte[n]dent.

lity of er— ply.

Experience has led us to regard as of paramount importance in the planting down of an insane colony or community in a given locality, the *quality* as well as the *quantity* of the water to be supplied for cooking and drinking. Especially is it important in regard to the material in which the said water is to be stored, or through which it is to be led. The material at present generally used for cisterns, and not unfrequently also for pipes, is lead. But this metal is apt to be acted on by various waters in such a way, and with such facility, as to give rise to two classes of serious dangers or disadvantages. Firstly, a portion of the lead—in the form of oxide and carbonate—may be gradually taken up by the water, either in a state of solution or suspension or both, and deleterious or even poisonous results may accrue to persons using it, according to the quantity so taken up by the water and swallowed by the person. This may be the unknown or unsuspected source of constant colicky and paralytic affections among the inmates of an Asylum. Secondly, the water may so act on the lead as to produce its frequent erosion to the extent of causing constant leakage. This necessitates the frequent repairs of lead cisterns or pipes, and at no long intervals sometimes the renewal thereof. It has long been generally accepted by chemists and by the public as a fact, that it is *soft* or pure waters which thus act on lead, and that they do so in proportion to their softness or purity. This is in the main correct; but it is not absolutely true, for some soft or pure waters do not thus act upon lead. But what is more important for us to announce is, that certain *hard* waters, under certain circumstances, act upon lead as powerfully, and in as deleterious a way, as certain pure or soft ones do. This was the conclusion to which we were led by a series of investigations or experiments made last year and laid before the meeting of the British Association at Leeds.* To the paper embodying the researches in question we must refer for full particulars of the circumstances under which the corrosive action of hard waters on lead takes place, as well as the various modes of preventing or remedying it. The reading of the said paper elicited from the chemists and scientific men present an expression of the opinion that *lead* must be considered, under all circumstances, a dangerous metal to use for the conveyance or storing of water, or at least one

ion of ters on l.

* "On the Action of Hard Waters on Lead:" Read before the Chemical Section of the British Association, September, 1858.—*Edinburgh New Philosophical Journal*, April, 1859.

which cannot be used without certain precautions. And it also drew forth the suggestion, that, in towns and communities of all sorts and sizes, before using a water for drinking or cooking purposes, great care should be taken to examine into its quality, as well as its quantity, particularly in reference to its action on the material to be used for its storing or conveyance. This, of course, can only be done by calling in the aid of experienced chemists. We are glad to observe that the Board of Lunacy gives a very useful and necessary advice or caution on this subject, in the suggestions regarding the construction of Asylums contained in their first Report (Appendix C, No. 1, Section 6, and No. 2, Section 30, Pp. 115 and 118). "It is of the utmost importance," say they, "that there should be a constant and ample supply of good water, of which a careful analysis should be made, with a view to determine the proper materials for pipes and reservoirs, and also in order to ascertain its fitness for the purposes of drinking and washing;" and, again, in reference to *rain water*, "*Lead* is an objectionable material for pipes and reservoirs as adulterating the water." Water should, if possible, be supplied by gravitation to the highest part of the building in every Asylum; failing this, steam power ought to be used to pump it up into large cisterns on or under the roof. It is fraught with many disadvantages to be compelled to have recourse—as is the case in some of the older Scotch Asylums—to manual labour—the work of patients—to drive the pumps, or otherwise manage the requisite machinery.

Importan of Chemi Analysis Waters.

Gravitati Supply *versus* Pumping.

We are gratified to find that the Board of Lunacy takes up substantially the same view with ourselves as to the great advantages of Asylums being of a composite character, and especially as to the usefulness of "adjunct houses," or separate buildings, of a cottage kind.* The fact of such an organisation of the new District Asylums being strongly recommended by Government, renders it extremely probable that it will be adopted in some of these Asylums at least. Indeed, we believe the District Boards of Scotland will lay themselves open to severe censure by the country if they do not follow out the spirit, if not the letter, of the enlightened suggestions of the Commissioners, to which we advert. But not only are we in favour of detached buildings for certain classes of patients—as the quiet, harmless, and industrious—but we should further recommend that the central or principal building—the hospital

Advantag of "Adjur Houses" a Cottages.

* First Annual Report, Appendix C, No. 2, Section 6.

proper—should consist, to a certain extent, of separate segments or departments, so as to permit of a proper classification of the inmates. Thus, it appears to us advisable to provide separate departments for—1. The excited, noisy, and violent; 2. The helpless, dirty, and paralytic; 3. The sick; and, 4. The epileptics. The department for the sick should admit of a greater degree of isolation than the other departments, so that it may become available in times of epidemic disease. But it would be inconvenient to allow such an invalid department to obviate the necessity of providing sick rooms or infirmaries in every gallery for the benefit of such patients as it is not necessary or advisable to have removed to a greater distance. The arrangement of the departments ought to be such as will admit of a comparatively complete separation or isolation, but which will not, at the same time, interfere with easy access to the officers of the establishment. Moreover, as a broad general principle, there ought to be a separation between the sleeping accommodation and the departments devoted to the purposes of parlours, dining saloons, workshops, reading-rooms, &c. The sleeping accommodation ought to be on a separate storey—on the second storey, namely—the apartments to be occupied during the day being on the ground storey. It is unnatural and unhomelike to have dormitories and parlours—night and day accommodation—associated so intimately as they are in the older Scotch Asylums; and the plan of separation above referred to is attended with many advantages. We believe that the best construction of an Asylum is one of two storeys—we mean for the advantage of the patients. Should there arise a necessity for its enlargement, and in every Asylum this must occur sooner or later, it is certainly more economical to extend in the direction of *height* by building a third storey. In this case, we think the third storey, as well as the second, should be set apart for sleeping accommodation. But in the interests of the patients, rather than of the ratepayers, we would recommend extension in the direction of *length* as the preferable arrangement.

There are few matters of more importance in the construction of an Asylum than the arrangements for heating and ventilation. Without reviewing the various means, which have been hitherto employed for these purposes, and which are generally more or less expensive, complex, and unsatisfactory or mischievous, we would simply strongly commend heating by means of open fireplaces, and ventilation by means of ordinary doors and windows.* We cannot have with the old system of flues both adequate heating and ventilation, nor can the distribution of the heat be at all times properly equalised or regulated. According as superintendents take different views of the relative advantages of heating and ventilation, so we find particular Asylums over-heated or under-heated. We believe overheating to be infinitely the greater danger of the two in public Asylums. In order at all to equalise the temperature, doors and windows must be kept closed; a stifling, hot atmosphere is produced; nausea and lassitude, coughs and colds, are complained of by the patients, who frequently of themselves request the flue-fires to be removed. We are not satisfied that any complex modern system of heating is at all comparable, in point of efficiency, with the old and simple plan of open fireplaces, which have the additional advantage of appearing comfortable, cheerful, and homelike. We prefer, infinitely, to see a group of patients reading or talking round a blithe fireside, rather than crouching round the opening of some flue, which is belching forth its gusts of hot, sickening air. Most Asylum Superintendents whom we have met, who have tried all the chief means of heating, or seen them tried, prefer hot water to hot air; but they are gradually giving up both in favour of ordinary open fireplaces. In connection with the subject of open fireplaces, we would caution the constructors of Asylums against altogether doing away with *fireguards*. We feel this caution absolutely necessary, in so far as the opinion is propagated by recognised authorities that they are quite unnecessary *under any circumstances*. We can only say that we tried the experiment of abolishing them, in deference to the opinion alluded to, and that we were speedily compelled to replace them, in some form, in the majority of cases. We found them more especially necessary on the female side of the house; in some cases, on account of epileptic patients being in the habit of sitting over the fire and falling into it occasionally while in a fit; in others, from patients deliberately setting fire to themselves, or to the property of other patients; in others, on account of patients sitting for long periods so near the fire as to burn their persons or clothing. Undoubtedly such accidents arise in some Asylums from the mixed character of the inmates of the galleries, and the impossibility, from limited

Dangers of Over-Heating.

Advantages of open Fire-places.

Use and Abuse of Fireguards

Accidents from Fire.

* Mr. Tite, M.P. recently stated in Parliament: "So far as I have observed, *all* artificial systems of ventilation are *a failure*. Whether you have to ventilate a large room or a House of Parliament, the best way is to *open a window*."

space, of segregating the epileptics, pyromaniacs, and other dangerous patients. But even could a proper classification be carried out, we believe it would be exceedingly unsafe to have open fireplaces without fireguards in the galleries or apartments set aside for epileptics, the excited and turbulent, and certain other classes of patients.

cupation Patients District ylums.

Mistakes may naturally arise as to the nature of the work at which patients should be employed in the new District Asylums. Directors are perhaps apt to suppose that the kind of work, which answers well in one Asylum, should answer equally well in another. This, however, is a great mistake. Practically, it will be found, that in one Asylum, weaving is most successfully and beneficially carried on; in another, spinning ropes or picking oakum; in a third, garden or field labour; in

riety in bour.

a fourth, carpentry, masonry, and other handicrafts. In Asylums near large towns, the handicrafts will probably be generally found to succeed best; while, in those in the centre of agricultural districts, field labour is most likely to be beneficial. The character of the work should be regulated partly by the prevalent occupations of the district in which the Asylum is situated—partly by the previous occupation of individual patients—partly by a consideration of the kind of work likely to be physically most suitable to particular patients. A *variety* of work is absolutely necessary. At the same time, there is no work so generally acceptable, none so serviceable to the physical health of the patients, as

ricultu- Labour.

field or garden work. Agricultural labour in a pauper Asylum is important in two distinct aspects—1st, as healthful to the patients; and, 2d, as remunerative to the establishment—a means of increasing its revenue, and thus assisting in the reduction of the rates of board and of

ofits of bour.

the burden on the ratepayer. Some authorities go the length of asserting that a pauper Asylum, with a sufficiency of farm land, should be self-supporting. But this is probably an extreme view, one based on the idea of economy or the interests of the ratepayer, rather than on that of cure or the interests of the patient. It should never be forgotten that the chief object of an Asylum is the cure and comfort of the insane, and all questions of economy or profit should be subsidiary or subservient to this grand aim and object. Fortunately, to a certain extent, but only to a certain extent, and the extent must be jealously considered, the interest of the ratepayers and the interest of the patients are identical in regard to the benefits to accrue from agricultural

tizan At- ndants.

labour. In the larger Pauper Asylums, and especially in those of country districts, we would strongly recommend the possession of a staff of artisan attendants—that is, attendants who have been brought up as carpenters, masons, plumbers, blacksmiths, tailors, shoemakers, and gardeners, whose labours would save a considerable outlay in procuring tradesmen from distant towns, and would otherwise be a great convenience, inasmuch as accidents are constantly occurring in a large establishment, which require the immediate repair of pipes, locks, doors, &c. These attendants would, moreover, superintend the workshops, and train the patients in various profitable handicrafts. *Gasmaking, baking,* and *brewing* are among the processes which it may be profitable or expedient to carry on in the larger pauper Asylums, particularly those considerably removed from towns. In small establishments, and especially those in the vicinity of large towns, these operations can scarcely be expected to prove remunerative; in the larger Asylums already existing, in England especially, they are being gradually introduced both as economical and as otherwise convenient. For the same reasons they are occasionally to be found carried on in the mansion-houses of country proprietors or landowners. It should not be forgotten that *steam*, and the mechanical appliances which may be made to work under its agency, may become available in a great variety of ways, as in ventilation, washing, cooking, gasmaking, pumping water, &c.; and it must be cause of regret if so powerful an agent is not taken advantage of as a means of saving manual labour. Again the principle of *railways* may be rendered extremely useful in the conveyance of supplies to, and of food from, the kitchen; while, by means of the *electric telegraph*, the Superintendent may flash his orders to every part of the colony or community under his charge. Indeed, there are many of the practical results of scientific discoveries and inventions during the last half-century which may be made of service in the construction or organisation of an hospital for the insane; we need not descend to details—it must suffice to indicate the direction in and from which assistance may be expected. Though their usefulness is obvious, *fire-engines* and *lightning-rods* are apt to be forgotten in the construction of large edifices. By certain modifications in, or additions to, the apparatus, the fire-engines might be made useful in cleaning the exterior of the building, airing courts or galleries, or in watering the fields or garden.

Gasmaking, Baking, and Brewing.

Applications of Steam Power.

Railways.

Electric Telegraph.

Fire-engines

Lightning-Rods.

Many of the older existing Asylums commit a great error in allowing the escape of their whole sewage, which, if collected for agricultural

Sewage Manure.

purposes, would be of great value. There is no difference of opinion among agricultural chemists as to the superior value of water-closet sewage and farmyard manure over guano, seaweed, fish, or artificial manures. It is impossible to calculate the vast resources deliberately squandered, recklessly thrown away, in the form of sewage, not only in our large towns, but in every farm or house which has a field, garden, or plot of ground attached to it. Fortunately, the District Asylums of Scotland will all possess farm lands of greater or less extent, and it would be an absurd and unpardonable waste of resources not to store up and render available the Asylum sewage. It is not our object here to show how this may best be done, nor are we the most competent authority to deal with such a subject, otherwise we might dwell, for instance, on the advantages of separating the solid from the liquid parts of the sewage, or on the mode of irrigating farm lands possessing a natural slope with the liquid portion thereof. What we are desirous of impressing on District Boards of Lunacy is, the conviction, that, with Asylum labour and Asylum sewage, Asylum farms, if properly managed, ought to become very productive, and that the more productive they are made, the greater will be the diminution of the rates of board for patients, and of the burden on the district, county, or parochial exchequer.

roductive-ess of arms.

iring ourts.

The possession of a multiplicity of small airing courts with high walls is another of the absurdities of the older Scotch Asylums. There is no necessity for more than one, or at most two, attached to each chief department of the Asylum, the male and female sides of the house. But they should be large, roomy, neatly laid out, with a good exposure, and having the ground sufficiently raised, or the walls sufficiently low, to place at the command of patients an extensive, cheerful view. Moreover, they should possess arcades or corridors provided with seats, for exercise or recreation in bad weather; substitutes, indeed, for the cage-like balconies that presently exist in several of the Scotch Asylums. British Asylums generally are deficient in covered arcades or corridors, but we have seen them of great use in some Continental ones, such as that of Christiania. In lieu of arcades or corridors, we would strongly recommend, as an admirable, though considerably more expensive, arrangement, courts covered with glass, admitting abundance both of air and light, which would be particularly serviceable in wet weather. They might be fitted up partly as conservatories, partly as aviaries,

rcades.

partly as gymnasia. It may seem an unnecessary luxury or refinement to propose attaching gymnasia to *Pauper* Asylums; but we do not hesitate to do so from a conviction of their usefulness. Perhaps, under a more humble designation, that of playground, they may appear less objectionable. We know of no reason why certain sections of patients, pauper or private, should not have their swings, skittles, or racket; racing, climbing, or leaping; boating, bathing, swimming; curling, skating, and so forth. So far as our opportunities have permitted, we have placed all these exercises or amusements at the command of our patients, with the result of still further encouraging us to extend our efforts in the same direction. In the great majority of cases, the physical constitution of an insane patient requires cultivation, and if our attention is not directed to this, as much as to the mental constitution, our efforts are little likely to prove satisfactory. Gymnasia or playgrounds, we readily admit, are not likely to be so much wanted or so serviceable in Pauper Asylums, as in those for the higher classes, inasmuch as the majority of patients in the former will probably be engaged in out-of-door or handicraft labour. But this is not a sufficient reason for their non-establishment, even in Pauper Asylums. There are always some patients to whom gymnastic exercises will be beneficial, not merely as amusements only: and the necessary appliances of a gymnasium need not be either complex or expensive. Gymnasia.

There are various conveniences within an Asylum which it may be thought superfluous to insist on the necessity of providing; only those, however, who have experienced the want of them can properly appreciate their great importance and usefulness. Architects are very apt to overlook what they regard as minor matters, but which are minor in no sense in which they can be regarded. The want of a sufficiency of such conveniences is a characteristic of most of the older Asylums we have visited, and unfortunately of certain new ones also, where architects alone have had to do with their construction. We allude particularly to—1. *Water-closets.* They should be numerous, large, well lighted and ventilated; in every gallery or department of the house; all in-doors; with unlimited water-supply for flushing; having provision against the misuse of the seats. They should never be used as sinks or sculleries. No self-acting system of flushing, however ingenious, is likely to prove permanently satisfactory: no plan for cleansing is so efficient and inexpensive ultimately as frequent periodical flushing by attendants. In the older Water-Closets.

Asylums, the airing courts are sometimes defiled with the presence of unsightly privies, an arrangement objectionable in the extreme. 2. Sculleries. *Sculleries;* with ample sinks for dirty water, conveniences and space for washing dishes, and presses for pails and brushes, &c.; they should be independent of, and in addition to, but in the vicinity of, the water-closets, lavatories, and bathrooms. They cannot be too numerous and capacious. Storerooms. 3. *Storerooms.* There should be two large storerooms, one on either side of the house, with abundant shelving or presses for classifying the clothing of patients, and for holding stocks of goods required in the tailor's and milliner's departments. A storeroom should be attached to the kitchen for holding groceries, bread, beer, and other victuals—said storeroom being independent of a meat-safe and dairy-room. Each gallery should, moreover, possess a storeroom, which may be also the attendants' room, for holding the clothing of the patients inhabiting such gallery. Presses. 4. *Presses* cannot be too abundantly distributed in every part of the houses; they are required for culinary utensils and crockery, bedding and towelling, pails, brooms and brushes, clothes, and endless *et ceteras.* Lavatories. 5. *Lavatories* should be attached to every department and gallery of the building; they should be roomy, well lighted, and well ventilated. A common fault in construction is to give each individual too little space for ablution, where several patients are washing themselves at the same time, as necessarily occurs every morning. The simplest taps or other appliances are the best: many most ingenious contrivances have been introduced calculated to attract the eye, but they all labour under the common objection, that they are constantly getting out of repair in proportion to their complexity of mechanism. Bath-Rooms 6. *Bath-rooms* should be provided in every gallery, possessing appliances for hot, cold, and shower baths. But, in addition, it is very desirable to possess two large bath-rooms—one for the male, and another for the female, side of the house—placed in a central situation, each Salle des Bains. being a sort of "Salle des Bains," provided with at least a dozen strong, durable baths. The trough-like baths of the older Scotch Asylums should not be imitated. As a general rule, the same form of bath which does for the sane answers for the insane.

In conclusion, we would, in addition to the "Suggestions and Instructions issued by the Board (of Lunacy for Scotland) in reference to —1. Sites; 2. Construction and Arrangement of Buildings; 3. Plans, of Lunatic Asylums," contained in Appendix C, page 115, of the first annual Report of the said Board,* take the liberty of directing the attention of all who are in any way concerned with the new District Asylums of Scotland, to an admirable series of propositions anent the construction and organisation of Asylums, "made by the Standing Committee of the Association of Medical Superintendents of American Institutions for the Insane, at its meeting in Philadelphia, May 21st, 1851;" and also at its meeting in Baltimore, May 10th, 1853, and published in the *American Journal of Insanity*.

* Published by Thomas Constable, publisher, Edinburgh, 1859.

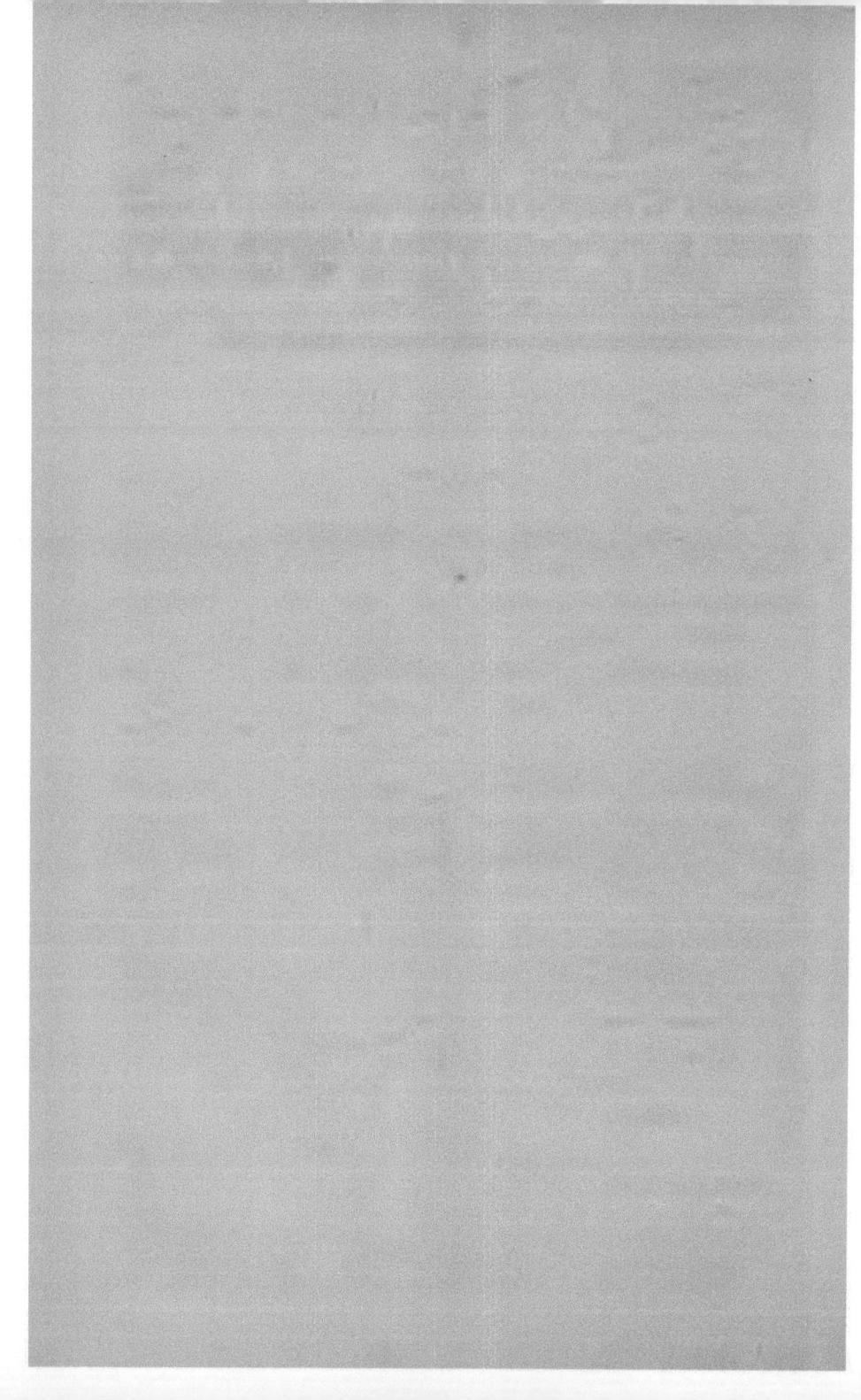

APPENDIX

TO

REPORT OF MEDICAL SUPERINTENDENT,

CONTAINING

STATISTICAL TABLES

RELATIVE TO

GENERAL RESULTS, ADMISSIONS, RECOVERIES, AND DEATHS.

I.—GENERAL RESULTS OF THE YEAR, 1858–9.

				Males.	Females	Total.
Patients admitted from 1827 to 1858. ...	...	...	...	564	566	1,130
	Males.	Females.	Total.			
Of these Recovered, ...	203	275	478			
„ Removed improved,	72	61	133			
„ „ unimproved,	74	59	133			
Died, ...	131	80	211			
				480	475	955
Patients remaining, June, 1858,	...	...	...	84	91	175
„ admitted during the year, June, 1858, to June, 1859,	...	...	...	37	42	79
Total number of Patients under treatment during 1858-9,...	...	...	...	121	133	254
	Males.	Females.	Total.			
Of these Recovered, ...	13	21	34			
„ Removed improved,	2	1	3			
„ „ unimproved,	1	4	5			
„ Died, ...	7	4	11			
				23	30	53
Patients remaining, June, 1859,	...	...	...	98	103	201

Mean daily number of Patients under treatment during 1858-9, 190.310.

II.—ADMISSIONS.

	Males.	Females.	Total.
1.—Age of Patients admitted.			
Between 15 and 20 years, ...	1	0	1
„ 20 „ 30 „	4	11	15
„ 30 „ 40 „	10	9	19
„ 40 „ 50 „	15	11	26
„ 50 „ 60 „	4	9	13
„ 60 „ 70 „	1	2	3
„ 70 „ 80 „	2	0	2
2.—Sex.			
Males, ...	37	0	79
Females, ...	0	42	
3.—Social Condition.			
Married, ...	12	12	24
Single, ...	23	22	45
Widowed, ...	2	8	10
4.—Occupation or Rank.			
Actress, ...	0	1	1
Baker, ...	1	0	1
Bootbinder, ...	0	2	2
Builder, ...	1	0	1
Butler, wife of a, ...	0	1	1
Cabinetmakers, ...	2	0	2
Carter, wife of a, ...	0	1	1
Clergyman's daughter, ...	0	1	1
Cooks, ...	0	2	2
Cooper, wife of a, ...	0	1	1
Dairywoman, ...	0	1	1
Draper, ...	1	0	1
Factory girls or women, ...	0	2	2
Farmers, ...	3	0	3
Farm-Servants, ...	4	5	9
„ , wife of a, ...	0	1	1
Flaxspinner, ...	0	1	1
Flaxdresser, ...	1	0	1
Gamekeeper, ...	1	0	1
Gardener, ...	1	0	1
Grocer, ...	1	0	1
Hawker, ...	0	1	1
Housekeepers, ...	0	2	2
Inland Revenue Officer, wife of an, ...	0	1	1

II.—ADMISSIONS—[Continued.]

	Males.	Females.	Total.
Ironmaster, ...	1	0	1
Labourer, ...	1	0	1
Mason, ...	1	0	1
Merchant, ...	1	0	1
„ wife of a, ...	0	1	1
None, ...	2	2	4
Nurse, ...	0	1	1
Officer in the Army, ...	1	0	1
Printer, ...	1	0	1
Quarryman, ...	1	0	1
Saddler, ...	1	0	1
Sailor, ...	1	0	1
„ wife of a, ...	0	1	1
Schoolmaster, ...	1	0	1
Servants, domestic, ...	0	7	7
Shoemakers, ...	3	0	3
„ wife of a, ...	0	1	1
Shopkeeper, ...	0	1	1
Slater, ...	1	0	1
Smith, ...	1	0	1
Tailors, ...	2	0	2
Teacher, ...	0	1	1
Weavers, ...	2	3	5
Writer to the Signet, widow of a, ...	0	1	1
5.—*Form of Insanity.*			
Dementia, ...	9	1	10
General Paralysis, ...	1	1	2
Mania, Acute, ...	7	10	17
„ Chronic, ...	1	3	4
„ Nymphomania, ...	0	2	2
„ Puerperal, ...	0	1	1
Melancholia, ...	8	16	24
Monomania, ...	11	8	19
6.—*Causes assigned.*			
Association with other insane members of family, ...	1	0	1
Congenital, ...	1	0	1
Desertion by husband, ...	0	2	2
Disappointment in love, ...	0	5	5
Dissipation, ...	1	0	1
Excitement in business, ...	3	0	3

II.—ADMISSIONS—[Continued.]

	Males.	Females.	Total.
Excitement in connection with celebration of Burns' Centenary, ...	1	0	1
Family bereavements or afflictions, ...	2	5	7
Fright, ...	0	1	1
Hereditary, ...	2	0	2
Ill-usage by husband, ...	0	4	4
Intemperance, ...	7	2	9
Jealousy, ...	2	0	2
Masturbation, ...	2	0	2
None assigned or known, ...	12	17	29
Over-study, ...	1	0	1
Parturition, ...	0	1	1
Quarrel, ...	1	0	1
Remorse regarding past conduct, ...	0	1	1
Religious excitement, ...	1	2	3
Scandal, ...	0	1	1
Sequelæ of Fever, ...	0	1	1
7.—*Co-existent physical disease or deformities, &c.*			
Cephalalgia, ...	0	1	1
Chronic vomiting, ...	1	0	1
Constipation, ...	1	1	2
Debility from abstinence, extreme, ...	0	2	2
„ other causes, ...	4	3	7
Distension of Mammæ, ...	0	1	1
Dyspepsia, ...	0	1	1
General Paralysis, ...	1	1	2
Hæmorrhoids, ...	1	1	2
Incontinence of Urine, ...	1	0	1
None, ...	23	23	46
Paraplegia, partial, ...	1	0	1
Pregnancy, ...	0	1	1
Salivation, ...	0	1	1
Strumous Diathesis, strongly marked, ...	1	5	6
Suicidal wounds (throat), ...	3	0	3
Synovitis Chronic (knee joint), ...	0	1	1
8.—*Duration of Disease prior to admission.*			
Under a week, ...	6	5	11
Between a week and a month, ...	5	11	16
„ 1 and 6 months, ...	7	13	20
„ 6 „ 12 „ ...	3	5	8

II.—ADMISSIONS—[Continued.]

	Males.	Females.	Total.
Between 1 and 2 years, ...	3	2	5
„ 2 „ 5 „	2	4	6
„ 5 „ 10 „	1	2	3
„ 10 „ 20 „	3	0	3
„ 20 „ 30 „	2	0	2
„ 30 „ 40 „	3	0	3
Congenital, ...	2	0	2
9.—*Re-Admissions: a. Frequency of recurrence or relapse.*			
For Second time, ...	2	4	6
„ Third „	3	3	6
„ Fifth „	0	1	1
b. Intervals of recurrence or relapse.			
Between 1 and 6 months, ...	1	1	2
„ 6 „ 12 „	0	3	3
„ 1 year and 5 years, ...	2	1	3
„ 5 „ 10 „	0	3	3
„ 20 „ 30 „	2	0	2
10.—*Suicidal and Homicidal propensities.*			
Homicidal, ...	1	3	4
Suicidal, ...	7	11	18
Suicidal and homicidal, ...	1	1	2

III.—RECOVERIES.

	Males.	Females.	Total.
1.—*Age.*			
20 years or under, ...	3	1	4
Between 20 and 30 years, ...	3	3	6
„ 30 „ 40 „	4	6	10
„ 40 „ 50 „	3	5	8
„ 50 „ 60 „	0	6	6
2.—*Sex.*			
Males, ...	13	0	} 34
Females, ...	0	21	

III.—RECOVERIES—[Continued.]

	Males.	Females.	Total.
3.—Social Condition.			
Married, ...	4	8	12
Single, ...	9	10	19
Widowed, ...	0	3	3
4.—Form of Insanity.			
Dementia, ...	1	0	1
Mania, Acute, ...	3	9	12
,, Puerperal, ...	0	1	1
Melancholia, ...	6	8	14
Monomania, ...	3	3	6
5.—Causes assigned.			
Annoyance about a legacy, ...	0	1	1
Desertion by husband, ...	0	2	2
Disappointment in love, ...	0	2	2
Embarrassment in business, ...	1	0	1
Family bereavements or afflictions, ...	1	3	4
Finding her house occupied by strangers,	0	1	1
Ill-usage by husband, ...	0	1	1
Intemperance, ...	2	1	3
Masturbation, sequelæ of, ...	1	0	1
Parturition, ...	0	1	1
Reading exciting tales, ...	1	0	1
Religious excitement, ...	2	0	2
Scandal, ...	0	1	1
Scarlatina, sequelæ of, ...	0	1	1
Suspicion or jealousy, ...	1	0	1
Unknown or not assigned, ...	4	7	11
6.—Duration of Disease prior to admission.			
One week or under, ...	3	5	8
Between 1 week and 1 month,... ...	0	7	7
,, 1 and 3 months, ...	6	5	11
,, 3 ,, 12 ,, ...	3	4	7
,, 2 ,, 10 years, ...	1	0	1
7.—Duration of treatment in Asylum.			
3 months or under, ...	3	7	10
Between 3 and 6 months, ...	4	6	10
,, 6 ,, 12 ,, ...	4	4	8
,, 1 ,, 2 years, ...	1	4	5
,, 2 ,, 5 ,, ...	1	0	1

III.—RECOVERIES—[Continued.]

The Recoveries constitute 64.15 per cent of the Discharges [including deaths.]
43.03 per cent of the Admissions.
17.86 per cent of the mean daily number of patients under treatment.
13.38 per cent of the total number under treatment during the year.

IV.—DEATHS.

	Males.	Females.	Total.
1.—*Age.*			
Between 30 and 40 years, ...	1	0	1
,, 40 ,, 50 ,, ...	2	1	3
,, 50 ,, 60 ,, ...	2	1	3
,, 60 ,, 70 ,, ...	0	1	1
,, 70 ,, 80 ,, ...	2	1	3
2.—*Sex.*			
Males—curable cases, ...	2	0	2
,, incurable cases, ...	5	0	5
Females—all incurable cases, ...	0	4	4
3. *Occupation or rank.*			
Clergyman, ...	1	0	1
Draper, ...	1	0	1
Factory worker, ...	0	1	1
Farmer, ...	1	0	1
Flax Dresser, ...	1	0	1
Labourer, ...	1	0	1
Nurse, ...	0	1	1
Servant, domestic, ...	0	1	1
Shoemaker, ...	1	0	1
Stock-Farmer, ...	1	0	1
Winder of Yarn, ...	0	1	1
4.—*Cause of death.*			
Apoplexy, simple, ...	0	1	1
,, in course of General Paralysis,	1	0	1
Broncho-Pneumonia, Acute, double, ...	1	0	1
,, with Acute Pleurisy,	1	0	1

IV.—DEATHS—[Continued.]

	Males.	Females.	Total.
Convulsions in course of General Paralysis,	0	1	1
Dysentery, ...	1	0	1
Pneumonia, double, Typhoid, ...	1	0	1
Senile Exhaustion, simple or uncomplicated,	1	0	1
" " fatal by Syncope, ...	0	1	1
" " complicated with Chronic Bronchitis, ...	1	0	1
" " complicated with Broncho-Pneumonia, ...	0	1	1
5.—Duration of Residence in Asylum.			
Between 1 and 6 months, ...	2	2	4
" 6 months and 1 year,... ...	1	1	2
" 1 year and 6 years, ...	1	0	1
" 12 " 15 "	0	1	1
" 15 " 20 "	1	0	1
" 20 " 40 "	2	0	2
6.—Form of Insanity.			
Dementia, ...	1	0	1
General Paralysis, ...	2	1	3
Mania, Acute, ...	1	0	1
" Chronic, ...	0	1	1
Melancholia, ...	1	2	3
Monomania, ...	2	0	2
7.—Period of death: a. Months or Seasons of the year.			
February, ...	1	0	1
April, ...	0	1	1
May, ...	1	0	1
July, ...	2	0	2
August, ...	0	1	1
September, ...	1	1	2
October, ...	0	1	1
December, ...	2	0	2
b. Hours of the day.			
Between midnight and 6, A.M.	2	2	4
" 6, A.M. and noon, ...	3	1	4
" 6, P.M. and midnight,... ...	2	1	3

IV.—DEATHS—[Continued.]

8.—Number of Deaths at or above the Age of 50, since 1827.

Age at Death.	Form of Disease.	M.	F.	Total.	
Between 50 and 60,	Dementia, ...	9	9	18	
	Mania, Acute, ...	6	2	8	
	„ Chronic, ...	1	2	3	
	Monomania, ...	2	0	2	
	Melancholia, ...	6	5	11	
	General Paralysis, ...	0	0	0·	
	Form of disease not mentioned,	4	2	6	
					48
Between 60 and 70,	Dementia, ...	9	3	12	
	Mania, Acute, ...	1	2	3	
	„ Chronic, ...	3	0	3	
	Monomania, ...	1	1	2	
	Melancholia, ...	4	1	5	
	General Paralysis, ...	2	0	2	
	Disease not mentioned, ...	0	0	0	
					27
Between 70 and 80,	Dementia, ...	6	5	11	
	Mania, Acute, ...	0	2	2	
	„ Chronic, ...	1	1	2	
	Monomania, ...	5	0	5	
	Melancholia, ...	1	0	1	
	General Paralysis, ...	0	0	0	
	Disease not mentioned, ...	0	0	0	
					21
Between 80 and 90,	Dementia, ...	2	1	3	
	Mania, Acute	1	2	3	
	„ Chronic, ...	0	0	0	
	Monomania, ...	0	0	0	
	Melancholia, ...	0	0	0	
	General Paralysis, ...	0	0	0	
	Disease not mentioned, ...	0	1	1	7
		64	39	103	103

The Deaths constitute 20.75 per cent of the Discharges.
13.92 per cent of the Admissions.
5.78 per cent of the mean daily number of patients under treatment.
4.33 per cent of the total number under treatment during the year.

CHAPLAIN'S REPORT.

For the three months during which he has held office, the Chaplain is glad to be able to give in a very favourable report. During that period the Sunday and Week-day Services have been regularly performed. The attendance at these is large and steady; on the male side the Chapel is quite full. The number of females is not quite so large as formerly, as several were removed from the Asylum in an improved state shortly after his appointment.

Nothing can exceed the propriety and attention displayed by nearly every one of the patients. It is truly gratifying to observe the hearty manner in which they engage in singing, the apparent pleasure with which they listen to the reading of Holy Scripture, and the earnestness with which they listen to the simple declaration of the truths of the Gospel. The Chaplain cannot forbear mentioning the pleasure it has given him to see the kindly and obliging disposition displayed by the patients towards each other; one way (not to mention more) in which this is shown is the care with which several seek out the Psalms, text, or portion of Scripture for those who cannot so readily do it themselves.

In his private intercourse with the patients, the Chaplain naturally finds himself standing on a more delicate and difficult footing than in his more public duties. In dealing with them individually it is necessary to proceed with proper caution, and, as far as possible, with just discrimination. In the cases of several there is no occasion for the least reserve. The difficulty arises when he meets with those who have a tendency to religious Monomania, and with them it is sometimes advisable to refrain from all conversation on religious subjects; but even amongst them different cases give rise to wholly different treatment.

The Chaplain is glad to be able to bear testimony to the care and vigilance displayed by the attendants in bringing the proper patients to the Chapel, and to the ready and willing attention he has received from all the officials in the discharge of his duties.

In performing these duties he feels profoundly the peculiarly solemn nature of the trust committed to him; and his earnest prayer is, that God, with whom nothing is impossible, may abundantly bless his efforts for the spiritual enlightenment of those attending his ministrations, and that they may all enjoy that "peace of God which passeth all understanding"—the sure result to those whose fellowship is with the Father of our Spirits, and with His dear son, Jesus Christ.